Constructions

By Debbie Croft

T0342748

Contents

The Oresund Bridge

The first time you see the Oresund Bridge, you will agree it is a spectacular sight.

The combined bridge and tunnel sections stretch an incredible 16.4 kilometres. They link the countries of Denmark and Sweden. These countries are members of the European Union, therefore, people do not need to show their passports when travelling between the two places. People travelling into Sweden from Denmark need to clear customs, however, those entering Denmark do not.

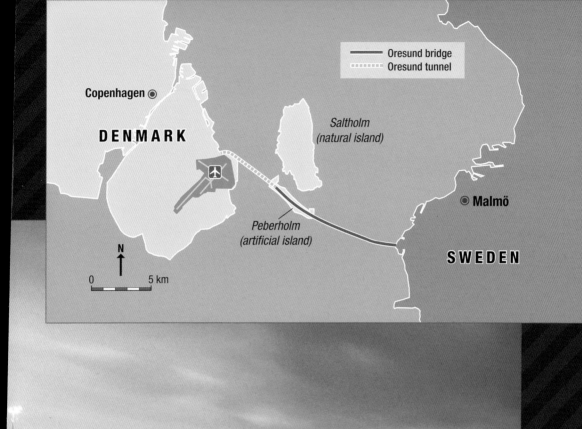

Copenhagen ⊙

DENMARK

Saltholm
(natural island)

Oresund bridge
Oresund tunnel

⊙ **Malmö**

Peberholm
(artificial island)

N

0   5 km

SWEDEN

Who would ever have thought that one day this large area of sea would cater for road and rail passengers? Yet the bridge and tunnel provide two rail tracks and a four-lane road bridge. Cars and trains can easily carry people from one country to another.

Instead of a 45-minute ferry ride, it takes only ten minutes to travel between the two countries. The bridge makes life much easier for people who live in one country and work in the other. Now they do not have to waste time travelling.

The bridge itself is the longest combined road and rail bridge in Europe. The main span is an amazing 1624 metres in length. It ends on an artificial island, then takes travellers into a four-kilometre long tunnel. This is the world's longest underwater tunnel.

It took four years to build the bridge. Its design looks plain, but the structure is quite complex. The two countries had hoped to build a bridge stretching across the water all the way from Denmark to Sweden. However, this span was too great. Adding a second bridge was not possible, because it would have been too close to the flight path of planes using Copenhagen Airport. So, the decision was made to combine a bridge with a tunnel.

Some of the main benefits of the bridge and tunnel are the opportunities it gives people to travel between the two countries more easily, share experiences and learn more about Denmark and Sweden.

Rosenberg Castle, Copenhagen, Denmark

the Turning Torso building and colourful houses, Malmö, Sweden

It doesn't matter whether you cross the bridge once in your lifetime or every day to go to work, you know you are taking a journey that you will remember for a long time.

Preserving Historical Buildings

There are strong opinions about the importance of historical buildings. Some people believe they should be pulled down and replaced with modern high-rise office blocks.

a historical area of Paris, Le Marais

the high-rise office area of Paris, La Défence

The Captain Cook Cottage was built in Yorkshire, England, in the eighteenth century and brought over to Melbourne in 1933.

But other people want governments to repair these buildings. They want them to last a long time because they believe the buildings are part of the history of the local area. If these buildings were pulled down, many people would not be able to learn about how their nation developed.

In some countries, early settlers constructed many of the historical buildings still standing today. People can learn about the construction skills that the settlers had. They can also see what materials the settlers used and can compare the designs used in earlier times with those used today.

Without these buildings, people may not know how families and workers lived in the past.

a pioneer cabin, Tennessee, USA

However, people who believe historical buildings should be pulled down put up strong arguments that say these buildings no longer have any value. They think it would be better to replace them with large, multi-storey office blocks. Land in major cities is extremely valuable. People say that each block should be used to cater for a large number of workers. Only a few people can work in a one-storey building.

the city skyline of Melbourne, Australia

In addition, it often costs a huge amount of money to repair historical buildings. Sometimes they are hundreds of years old. Many of them have become run down, and are beyond repair. Some people argue that it would be better to use the money to build new office blocks or apartment buildings.

modern buildings towering over old buildings, Guizhou, China

To summarise, there will most likely be ongoing debate about the future of historical buildings. Many people describe the past as having shaped the future. Others just as firmly believe that we cannot live in the past.

a traditional Japanese hut, Akita Prefecture, Japan

Whichever side of the argument you agree with, it is important to understand that these buildings helped nations to develop over hundreds of years.

office buildings and shops in the Shinjuku district of Tokyo, Japan